ATTACK OF THE ZOMBIE NITS

Alexander peered through the microscope at the teeming micro-organisms that filled the Petri dish.

'It's like nothing I've ever seen before!' he said, concerned. Raising his head, he gestured for James to take his place. 'Have a look.'

James hesitated. 'What's the point in me having a look?' he asked. 'I'm so good at chemistry I set fire to my tie with a Bunsen burner in the last exam!'

'I think you'll be interested in this,' said Alexander, stepping aside.

James peered through the eyepiece of the microscope for a second before looking up, his face pale.

'They look like little ghosts,' he said.

'*Exactly*,' replied Alexander. 'A

one place bacteria like th

'The plague pit,' sai

St Sebastian's School in Grimesford is the pits. No, really – it is.

Every year, the high school sinks a bit further into the boggy plague pit beneath it and, every year, the ghosts of the plague victims buried underneath it become a bit more cranky.

Egged on by their spooky ringleader, Edith Codd, they decide to get their own back – and they're willing to play dirty. *Really* dirty.

They kick up a stink by causing as much mischief as in inhumanly possible so as to get St Sebastian's closed down once and for all.

But what they haven't reckoned on is year-seven new boy, James Simpson and his friends Alexander and Lenny.

The question is, are the gang up to the challenge of laying St Sebastian's paranormal problem to rest, or will their school remain forever frightful?

There's only one way to find out . . .

www.too-ghoul.com

B. STRANGE

EGMONT

Special thanks to:

**Tommy Donbavand, St John's Walworth Church of
England Primary School and Belmont Primary School**

EGMONT
We bring stories to life

Published in Great Britain 2007
by Egmont UK Limited
239 Kensington High Street, London W8 6SA

Text & illustrations © 2007 Egmont UK Ltd
Text by Tommy Donbavand
Illustrations by Pulsar Studios (Beehive Illustration)

ISBN 978 1 4052 3239 5

1 3 5 7 9 10 8 6 4 2

A CIP catalogue record for this title is available
from the British Library

Typeset by Avon DataSet Ltd, Bidford on Avon, Warwickshire
Printed and bound in Great Britain by the CPI Group

'I really love *Too Ghoul for School* – I hope more books come out soon! My favourite character is Lenny cos he's hilarious!'

Jack, age 8

'Horribly disgusting five-star books. Don't stop making them!'

Owen, age 9

'Disgusting and good at the same time . . .'

Daniel, age 10

'I like the way the really horrible parts are in really good detail'

Charlie, age 10

'The books are great. I thought Edith Codd was REALLY funny. Ha, ha!'

Anthony, age 9

We want to hear what *you* think about *Too Ghoul for School*! Visit:

www.too-ghoul.com

for loads of cool stuff to do and a whole lotta grot!

School versus...

Year-seven new boy
and chief spook-hunter

James Simpson

Headmaster's son
and official brainiac

Alexander Tick

Strong as an ox,
gentle as an
unusually tall lamb

Lenny Maxwell

...Ghoul!

Loud-mouthed ringleader of the plague-pit ghosts

Edith Codd

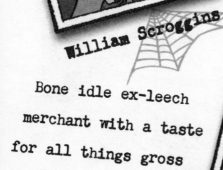

Young ghost and a secret wannabe St Sebastian's pupil

William Scroggins

Bone idle ex-leech merchant with a taste for all things gross

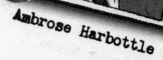

Ambrose Harbottle

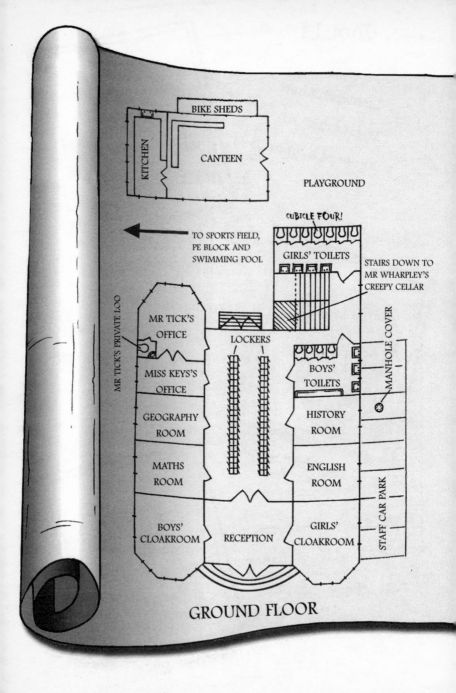

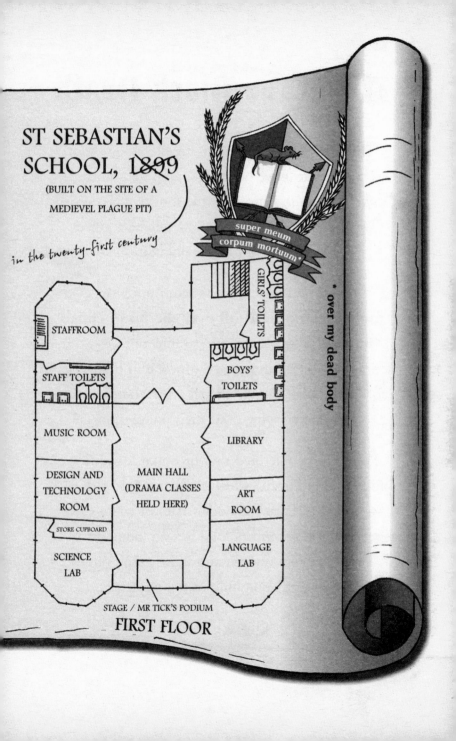

About the Black Death

The Black Death was a terrible plague that is believed to have been spread by fleas on rats. It swept through Europe in the fourteenth century, arriving in England in 1348, where it killed over one third of the population.

One of the Black Death's main symptoms was **foul-smelling boils all over the body called 'buboes'**. The plague was so infectious that its victims and their families were locked in their houses until they died. Many villages were abandoned as the disease wiped out their populations.

So many people died that graveyards overflowed and bodies lay in the street, so special **'plague pits'** were dug to bury the bodies. Almost every town and village in England has a plague pit somewhere underneath it, so watch out when you're digging in the garden . . .

Dear Reader

As you may have already guessed, B. Strange is not a real name.

The author of this series is an ex-teacher who is currently employed by a little-known body called the Organisation For Spook Termination (Excluding Demons), or O.F.S.T.(E.D.). 'B. Strange' is the pen name chosen to protect his identity.

Together, we felt it was our duty to publish these books, in an attempt to save innocent lives. The stories are based on the author's experiences as an O.F.S.T.(E.D.) inspector in various schools over the past two decades.

Please read them carefully - you may regret it if you don't . . .

Yours sincerely
The Publisher.

PS - Should you wish to file a report on any suspicious supernatural occurrences at your school, visit **www.too-ghoul.com** and fill out the relevant form. We'll pass it on to O.F.S.T.(E.D.) for you.

PPS - All characters' names have been changed to protect the identity of the individuals. Any similarity to actual persons, living or undead, is purely coincidental.

CONTENTS

CHAPTER 1
RIGHT ON QUEUE

'Where's the best place for a sickroom at school?' asked Alexander Tick in the lunchtime queue. Without pausing for a reply, he delivered the punchline: 'Right next to the canteen!'

Pupils around him groaned and turned away. His friends, James Simpson and Lenny Maxwell, shared a glance.

'It's bad enough that we have to queue up for twenty minutes every day,' moaned James. 'Don't feel you have to entertain us as well.'

'Oh, it's no problem!' beamed Alexander, missing

James's point entirely. 'I've got dozens of school-dinner jokes in my humour database, and I memorised them all this morning.'

A cry of despair echoed out along the lunch queue at the news.

'Did you hear about the cruel dinner lady?' he asked, glancing up and down the line for a willing victim to aim the rest of the joke at. 'She beat the eggs and whipped the cream!'

Lenny sighed. 'If it wasn't for the fact that my stomach thinks my mouth's on strike, I'd be racing in terror across the sports field right now,' he said.

'If you decide to head out that way, do us all a favour and take Stick with you,' said James. 'You could bury him in the sand pit at the long jump.'

'Oh, here's a good one . . .' began Alexander.

Once again, the queue let out a collective moan. James spun round and glared at him.

'You're not winning us any friends here, you know,' he hissed.

Alexander shrugged. 'Who needs friends when you've got an audience?' James shook his head and turned away. 'What kind of food do maths teachers eat?' continued Alexander.

Suddenly, the very large and very angry figure of Gordon 'The Gorilla' Carver forced his way back through the queue and grabbed Alexander's collar, shoving him hard against the wall. 'You finish that joke and I'll push your teeth so far down your throat you'll have to sit on your chips to chew them!' he threatened.

'G-Gordon!' stammered Alexander. 'You're not a comedy fan then?'

The Gorilla scratched his head and snarled. 'Oh, I like comedy,' he spat. 'I just don't like the rubbish you spout!'

'Well, it is a very s-subjective medium,' smiled Alexander as the bully pressed him harder against the wall. 'Th-the word "subjective" means some people like it, and others don't,' he explained.

James turned away, unable to watch. 'Does he
actually *want* to spend the rest of term in
hospital?' he asked Lenny.

'Why, thank you,' leered Gordon sarcastically, scratching at his scalp again and pressing his face into Alexander's. 'The question is, do you know what the word "pain" means?'

'Well, the dictionary describes "pain" as –' began the reply.

'*Alexander!*' yelled James and Lenny together.

'Oh,' said their friend, realising that he was just seconds away from yet another beating at the hands of The Gorilla.

'Look, Carver,' said James, stepping into the bully's line of sight. 'I'll make sure he doesn't tell any more jokes. Just let him go and I'll buy you an extra dessert, OK?'

Gordon's eyes drifted out of focus briefly as he considered the offer then, with a grunt, he released Alexander's collar and began to push his way back to his place at the head of the queue, scratching at his head once more.

James spun round to face Alexander. '*Now* will

you keep quiet?' he demanded. 'Not only have you just cost me the price of a rhubarb crumble, you've even managed to annoy Gordon's nits!'

The entire canteen fell silent as Gordon stopped, mid-scratch, and slowly turned around. 'What did you say?' he roared.

James became aware that other pupils were stepping away from him, clearing a path for The Gorilla to advance. 'I-I didn't . . .' he stuttered.

Gordon lurched forwards, grabbing a scoop of ice cream from a bowl on a nearby table and hurling it at James. The dessert's original owner opened her mouth to complain, then saw The Gorilla's face and thought better of it.

The ice cream landed with a 'splat' on James's shoulder, and the lunch queue erupted in laughter; laughter which stopped short when a blob of custard hit Gordon square in the face. Everyone turned to see Lenny looking sheepish.

'What did you do that for?' whispered James.

'Seemed like a good idea at the time,' Lenny replied.

With a howl, Gordon raced forwards, snatching a handful of mashed potato from the plate of a year-nine girl. He jumped on Lenny, rubbing it into the boy's face. Alexander and James leapt into action, pulling food from other tables and hurling it at the back of Gordon's head.

Within seconds, the entire canteen had erupted into a massive food fight. Cold chips, blackened sausages and tasteless peas flew everywhere as the pupils finally had the courage to treat the school menu with the respect it deserved.

The door to the kitchen burst open, and two dinner ladies raced out, ducking to avoid being covered with lumpy gravy.

'Stop this *right now*!' roared Mrs Cooper.

'We *slaved* over this food!' bellowed Mrs Meadows.

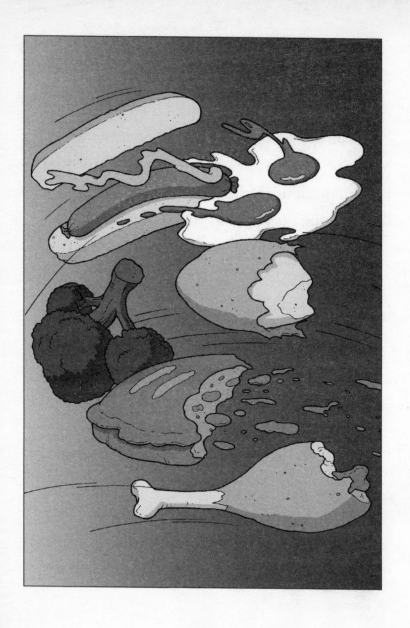

At this, the attack switched to the original source of the foul food – the dinner ladies. The two women scuttled across the canteen, hands over their heads, as they were pelted with soggy vegetables and slices of tough beef.

Reaching the centre of the battle, the dinner ladies pulled Lenny and Gordon apart.

'You're going straight to the headmaster's office!' shouted Mrs Cooper, as a glob of custard hit the back of her neck.

'You two as well!' added Mrs Meadows, grabbing James and Alexander before they could hurry away.

'What have *I* done?' moaned Alexander.

Mrs Meadows spat out a mouthful of limp carrot. 'We have to stand behind that counter every day listening to your so-called jokes!' she cried. 'It's payback time!'

Braving a fresh rain of school food, the two dinner ladies dragged the boys towards the canteen doors. As he was marched away, Alexander wiped cold gravy from his eyes and smiled.

'You know, this reminds me of the teacher who ordered a different school dinner every day of the year . . .' he began.

James pulled a handful of mashed turnip from his hair and forced it into Alexander's mouth, silencing him.

'I knew this stuff was good for something,' he muttered.

CHAPTER 2
WHAT A NIT

Miss Keys, the school secretary, sighed as
she dragged a flashing heart icon across her
computer screen and dropped it into place on the
Mr Tick web site she was designing. She couldn't
decide between www.worldsbestheadmaster.com
or www.mrtickislovely.com for a domain name,
so for the moment she was content to spend her
days adding pictures of her boss to the site's
'Hunky Headmaster' photo gallery.

Suddenly the door to her office burst open and
the two food-splattered dinner ladies marched

the grumbling boys into the room.

Miss Keys grabbed for her computer mouse to try and close down the site before anyone could see what she was working on, but all she managed to do was knock it down the back of her desk where it dangled, just out of reach. The secretary

stared in terror at the photo

swimming trunks that she ho

staff relay race at last year's so

gala. She leapt to her feet to bl

view of her monitor.

'Can . . . Can I help you?' she

back against the screen while stretching an arm

behind her to try and grab the cord of her mouse.

'These boys need to be disciplined!' announced

Mrs Cooper, as she extracted a lump of parsnip

from behind her ear. 'Look what they did to us!'

'And it's not just us!' added Mrs Meadows.

'The whole canteen is covered in food. It'll take

us forever to clean it up!'

'Oh, come on,' said Alexander, 'all you have to

do is shovel the mess back into the serving trays

for tomorrow's lunch.'

James nudged him hard in the ribs with an

elbow, and he yelped.

'Sort them out!' snapped Mrs Cooper as she

...der a dirty look and stomped out of ...m, closely followed by Mrs Meadows.

'Right ...' began Miss Keys, abandoning her search for the computer mouse and stretching out a hand for her telephone.

The boys watched as she twisted her body round, still desperating trying to keep the images on the computer monitor hidden. She managed to pull the telephone receiver from its cradle and drag it towards her with the ends of her fingernails.

Smiling brightly at the bemused boys, she tucked the receiver under her chin and reached out again to press a button on the phone. A tinny voice barked 'Yes?'

'Mrs Cooper has brought some boys in to see you, sir,' Miss Keys said, smiling. She listened for a second before nodding and moving the receiver away from her ear. 'Mr Tick says he'll be with you in a moment.'

Remembering the telephone was still out of

reach, she sighed. To her audience's amazement, the secretary tried to throw the receiver back into place. It missed, knocking a seaside souvenir mug filled with pencils off the desk and smashing it.

'Can I help you, Miss Keys?' asked Lenny.

'No, no . . . I'll get it later,' she beamed.

Silence filled the office for a moment before a beeping tone signalled that the phone was off the hook.

The four boys stared as Miss Keys gave out a small sob. She extended her leg and, looping the cord over her foot, she managed to flip the telephone receiver back on to the desk, scattering a box of paper clips in the process.

Satisfied, Miss Keys smiled and placed her hands back on the desk, catching one of the keys on her computer keyboard and accidentally playing a sound clip of the headmaster announcing, 'Red ace on black two to win!'

'Was that my dad's voice?' asked Alexander.

Miss Keys shook her head furiously. 'N-no,' she stammered. 'It was me!' Lowering her voice and attempting to sound like a man, she added: 'Sometimes Mr Tick asks me to make calls on his behalf.'

Gordon Carver scratched at his head and exchanged a puzzled glance with Alexander. The bully then joined the school secretary in wishing that Mr Tick would hurry up and let them in.

Inside his office, Mr Tick gazed at his reflection in the mirror as he ran a novelty comb shaped like a playing card through his thinning hair. 'I'll be the best-looking contestant at the solitaire championships in Norwich,' he told himself happily.

The intercom buzzed again. 'Yes?' he said, pressing the flashing red button on his telephone.

'I, er . . . really need you to let these boys in, Mr Tick!' announced Miss Keys through the speaker.

The headmaster harrumphed and reached for the office door. Pulling it open he was amazed to see his son and three other boys, each coated in crusty food, staring up at him. Behind them, Miss Keys was lying across her desk, arms and legs at awkward angles.

'Come in,' Mr Tick commanded. As he closed the office door behind them, there was a scream and a crash as Miss Keys finally toppled and fell off the desk.

The headmaster sat in his chair and peered over his glasses at the four boys. 'Now,' he began, 'why has Mrs Cooper sent you to see me?'

All four boys began to talk at once. Mr Tick tried to listen to each in turn, but could only make out the odd phrase: '. . . pelted me with mashed potato . . .', '. . . threw ice cream at me . . .', and '. . . wouldn't know funny if he fell over it!'

'One at a time!' roared the headmaster, silencing the lunch-spattered pupils.

'Dad, it's not our fault –' said Alexander, but Mr Tick raised a hand to stop him.

'May I remind you that between the hours of nine in the morning and three-twenty in the afternoon I am *not* your father, but your *headmaster*.'

Alexander sighed. 'Headmaster, it's not our fault!' he said. 'The Gorilla just attacked me because I was trying to lighten the mood in the canteen with a few jokes!'

'The Gorilla?' asked Mr Tick, leaning back in his chair.

'Alexander means Gordon Carver, sir,' said James.

Mr Tick turned his attention to the bully.

'Carver,' demanded the headmaster, glaring at Gordon, 'what have you got to say for yourself, boy?'

The Gorilla didn't reply. He simply stared, open-mouthed, and scratched furiously at his scalp.

'No need to scratch your head, Carver – it's a simple enough question!' bellowed Mr Tick. 'What happened in the school canteen?'

James, Lenny and Alexander watched in surprise as Carver continued to scratch at his head and made a noise that sounded like 'Nnnggh!'

'Carver?' said Mr Tick, rising from his chair and moving around the desk. He stopped a few feet away from the bully and peered down at his hair.

'By the knave of diamonds!' hissed the headmaster. 'You've got nits!'

Alexander snorted back a laugh. 'We could have told you that!'

'Then why didn't you?' demanded the headmaster. 'You have a duty as my son –'

Alexander raised a hand to silence his father. 'May I remind you that between the hours of nine in the morning and three-twenty in the afternoon I am not your son, but one of your pupils,' he smiled.

Mr Tick fought the urge to explode and snatched up the telephone receiver. 'In a case like this, there is only one person to call,' he said.

Alexander paled. 'Oh, no!' he groaned.

'What's wrong?' asked James. 'Who's he calling?'

Alexander gritted his teeth. 'Granny Tick!'

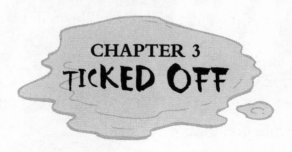

CHAPTER 3
TICKED OFF

Mr Downe, the religious studies teacher, placed his briefcase on the ground as he bent to drink from the water fountain. However, as the water touched his lips, he became aware of a bitter taste.

He ran the water around his mouth, letting his tongue swim in it. No, it wasn't the water that tasted wrong – it was the air. Something acidic, like the scent of dead flowers, was filling the corridor.

Suddenly, a shadow fell across the fountain and Mr Downe froze. He knew that shape; that

short, dumpy frame with a small medical bag
clutched tightly in one hand. Add it to the bitter
taste in the air and that could only mean one
thing: she was back!

He lifted his head slowly and squinted towards

the doorway where a figure stood, silhouetted against the bright sunlight. Instantly Mr Downe was transformed from a teacher with six years' experience at St Sebastian's to a clumsy, twelve-year-old schoolboy waiting in line to have his head checked for nits.

The teacher began to tremble as the figure stepped towards him, the ground almost shaking under her feet.

Mr Downe clamped a hand to his balding head. 'No!' he yelped. 'I don't have hair any more. You can't comb me!'

Throwing a sneer at Mr Downe, the figure lumbered past in the direction of Mr Tick's office.

The teacher crumpled to the floor beside the water fountain, where he was found by a group of year-nine pupils half an hour later, cuddling his briefcase.

William Scroggins floated up from the loo in the boys' toilets and looked around for his friends. Being a ghost certainly had its advantages; he didn't have to bother with doorways for one. It did mean, however, that the friends he was searching for didn't know of his existence.

William had died of the bubonic plague over six hundred years ago. He'd been eleven then and learning hadn't seemed important when he was alive. Now he was dead, William wanted nothing more than to be a pupil at St Sebastian's.

An older ghost, Ambrose Harbottle, seeped out of a vent in the wall, wincing as he heard a distant, strangled howl echo through the pipe work that led from the sewer below.

Both knew that angry scream of frustration anywhere: it was Edith Codd, leader of the plague-pit ghosts who'd made the sewer their home. William shivered, deciding to stay above ground with Ambrose, away from Edith and her crazed plans to close down the school for as long as she could.

Turning the corner, he was delighted to spot his friends – James, Lenny and the boy he looked uncannily similar to, Alexander – waiting patiently in a long queue outside the headmaster's office.

'I wish my dad had let us stay in his room,' he heard Alexander say as the boys glanced up at the closed door. 'I want to know what's going on in there!'

No problem! thought William, resisting the urge to become solid and reveal himself to the line of pupils. *Your wish is my command.* Patting his pal on the back with an ethereal hand, he floated through the wall and into Mr Tick's office.

Ambrose, remaining invisible to the children in the corridor, shook his head.

The headmaster of St Sebastian's paced nervously around his desk before finally looking at the figure sitting in his chair. William floated through the wall and perched on top of the filing cabinet to watch.

'I can't *believe* you let this happen!' bellowed Granny Tick, the headmaster's mother. 'Head lice – in your school! I thought you were more careful, Dickie!'

Dickie Tick! William giggled to himself.

'Mother, please don't call me Dickie on school property!' whined Mr Tick. 'It's Richard, and I didn't *let* anything happen – one of the pupils must have brought them in from home.'

Granny Tick harrumphed as she opened the battered, leather medical case that sat on the desk in front of her. 'It doesn't matter how they got here,' she sneered. 'What matters now is getting rid of them.'

She reached into the bag and pulled out a

26

fierce-looking metal comb which glinted in the
sunlight. William let out an involuntary gurgle
of fear.

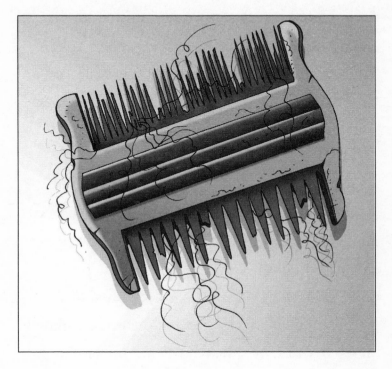

'Ah . . .' beamed Granny at the sound, 'it appears
my first victim is ready! Open the door, Dickie!'

Mr Tick sighed and trudged towards the office
door. William watched in horror.

'I can't let this woman loose on my friends!' he said to himself. 'I don't know what she'll do to them!'

He closed his eyes and concentrated hard. Instantly he was outside in the corridor with Ambrose, floating into his ghostly friend's body.

'What are you doing?' demanded Ambrose, as William's ectoplasm began to merge with his own.

'Just bond with me and I'll explain later!' hissed William.

The pair solidified and became one, resulting in a short figure with William's body and Ambrose's head.

Mr Tick opened the office door to find quite possibly the ugliest child he had ever seen standing at the front of the queue. 'Who are you?' he asked.

'He's first in line, that's who!' grinned Stuart Dixon, relieved at having switched places. Now there was someone willing to go before him, his mood had brightened considerably.

'Well, in you go! Have fun!' Stuart said, as he pushed the figure inside the headmaster's office.

'Why aren't you in school uniform?' demanded Mr Tick, as the William–Ambrose mixture took its place before Granny Tick, focusing hard on remaining as solid as possible.

'I was, er . . . rehearsing for the school play!' blurted William through Ambrose's rubbery lips. 'This is just a costume!'

Shame you didn't think to apply more make-up, thought the headmaster, staring in disbelief at Ambrose's pockmarked face. The older ghost smiled back, nervously.

'Up to your usual standard, I see,' moaned Granny Tick as she studied the combination of puny child and aged leech merchant who stood before her.

Mr Tick sighed. 'I can't be held responsible for the attractiveness of my pupils!' he countered, wincing as he watched his mother lay out the rest of her nit-combing equipment on his solitaire mouse mat. He made a brief mental note to find out why Mr Thomas, the drama teacher, hadn't informed him of any new productions and to ask Miss Keys how such an ugly child had made it on to the school register.

'Hold still, this shouldn't hurt,' said Granny Tick as she began to scrape the sharp teeth of the metal comb through William's unruly crop of dirty blond hair, now sitting on top of Ambrose's wrinkled scalp. 'But if it does, you'll just have to put up with it!'

William grinned inwardly as the older woman searched his hair roughly for evidence of head lice. She yanked his head from side to side, clipping clumps of it together with metal clamps and scraping his scalp with pointed skewers.

'Nope!' she announced after a while. 'Not a single nit! It's almost as though this boy contains no blood for them to feed on.'

Looking disappointed, she pushed the ugly boy away. 'You'd better not have called me here for nothing, Dickie!' she complained.

'There *are* nits, honest, Mum!' whinged the headmaster as he opened the door for William to leave. 'I've seen them!'

William smiled through Ambrose's mouth at Stuart as he trudged past him into the office, his fate having only been stalled for a few, brief moments.

'It's not so bad!' he tried to reassure him.

The rest of the queue didn't share his optimism as the door closed and, a few seconds later, Stuart Dixon screamed out in pain.

CHAPTER 4
SHAM-POOH!

'You idiot, Tick!' yelled Gordon down the queue of pupils outside the headmaster's office. 'If it wasn't for your stupid family, we wouldn't be waiting to have our scalps scraped raw!'

The other pupils in the queue grumbled in agreement.

'It's not Alexander's fault!' replied James. 'You're the one who brought nits into the school.'

'And they would have stayed on my head where they belong, but that little idiot went and told jokes in the canteen!' roared The Gorilla.

'Now we've got to put up with his gruesome granny as well as him and his dad!'

'And I say you're next, Carver!' came a shout from the office doorway. The headmaster glared down the line towards Gordon, as a sobbing year-nine girl squeezed past him with one hand pressed to her scalp and the other clutching a purple bottle of anti-nit lotion.

Gordon Carver left his place in the queue and shuffled towards the office door, much to everyone's amusement.

'Nitty Nora's going to have a field day with The Gorilla's head,' whispered James.

'The "Nitty Nora" you refer to happens to be my grandmother,' interrupted Alexander.

James shrugged a half-hearted apology.

'You're right though,' continued the headmaster's son as the office door closed and Gordon disappeared from view. 'He's about to be scraped, scratched, scored and scrubbed.'

'Thousands of nits will die,' said James, pulling a finger across the front of his throat dramatically.

'*Die?*' asked Lenny, fighting back tears at the news that living creatures, no matter how small and disgusting, were about to meet their doom. 'Your granny's going to *kill* them?'

Alexander stared at his tall friend, searching his face for some sign that he was joking. 'What did you think she was going to do with the head lice that she finds?'

'I don't know,' admitted Lenny. 'Release them back into the wild?'

'Look, it would be impossible!' snapped Alexander.

'But why?' asked Lenny.

'Because you'd have to make the cages really, really tiny!' said the headmaster's son.

'So?' continued Lenny. 'Humans can do all sorts of things these days with the help of modern technology. Artificial hearts . . . face transplants . . . Why not tiny cages?'

Alexander turned to James. 'You explain it to him before my head explodes!' he said.

'We understand you're upset, Lenny,' said James. 'But the practicalities of collecting all the "refugee head lice", as you're calling them, and setting them free elsewhere simply can't be overcome.'

'I just don't see why thousands of innocent creatures should die at the hands of this cruel and uncaring system!' said Lenny.

'It's not a system!' shouted Alexander. 'It's my granny!'

'She's still cruel and uncaring,' mumbled Lenny. Another scream echoed out of the headmaster's office. 'See?'

William and Ambrose, separated again, floated out of the corridor wall and studied the lengthy queue.

'I'm thinking about going in again,' said the younger ghost.

'Well, you can leave me out of it,' moaned Ambrose, chewing on a leech. 'It took me twenty minutes to get my body back into shape!'

'Don't be a grump!' teased William. 'It was fun!'

Ambrose swallowed hard, enjoying the sensation of a not-quite-dead-yet leech wriggling as it slid down his gullet. 'Great fun?' he asked. 'What was fun about having my scalp searched for insects?'

'It's not the fact that I had my hair looked at,' explained William. 'It's that I was there, in the office, being treated like a *real* pupil!'

Ambrose clamped a hand over the younger spirit's mouth. 'Don't you let Edith hear you saying that!' he hissed. 'She'll have you cleaning up rat poo for the next hundred years!'

'Relax!' smiled William. 'I checked – she's down in the sewers trying to train rats to bite people's bottoms. Now, come on – I want to find out what's in those purple bottles!'

Ambrose pulled another leech from his pocket, this one being long dead and very stiff. Sucking on it like a lollipop, he glided along the corridor after his enthusiastic young friend.

Behind him, a crooked, wart-covered nose and then a pair of crazed eyes appeared through the wall. 'St Sebastian's, your bottoms are safe from rat bites for the moment,' cooed Edith Codd as she studied the queue for the nit nurse. 'I've just had a better idea!'

'No, absolutely not!' spat the ghost of Aggie Malkin as she sniffed for a second time at the foul-smelling contents of the purple bottle. 'I do *not* concoct evil spells and potions!'

'Then what sort of witch *are* you?' screamed
Edith, her voice bouncing around the walls of
the vast amphitheatre that lay beneath the
school. 'Surely it's part of the job?'

Edith had ordered the cavern to be created by
the plague-pit ghosts so she'd have somewhere to
hold meetings, rants and general ravings. This
particular outburst, however, was more of a seethe.

'This is a perfect opportunity to rid ourselves of the school children forever!' continued Edith, snatching back the bottle and waving it in front of Aggie's face. 'They've all been told to wash their hair with this stuff. If we replace it with poison, they'll be wiped out before you can say "ectoplasm"!'

'I won't do it!' countered the witch. 'I managed to get through life without harming a child and I refuse to hang a black mark over my death by doing it now!' With that, she turned and stormed out of the cavern, leaving Edith alone.

'You plague-ridden old fool!' she screamed as the witch vanished into one of the sewer pipes. 'I don't need you! I can do it myself!'

Edith lifted her upturned barrel-cum-ranting post to reveal a collection of potion ingredients she'd hoarded over the centuries.

'I *knew* these would come in handy sometime,' she smiled, as she crouched over a puddle and began to drop globs of slime and lumps of rat droppings into the rancid water.

The king of clubs clock struck midnight in Mr Tick's office as Edith eased her way up through the U-bend of the headmaster's private toilet. Dragging the old, discarded bin liner up through the pipes had proved difficult. It sloshed noisily as Edith finally pulled it out of the toilet and dropped it on to the polished floor. She looked around.

On the desk, Granny Tick's nit combs gleamed sharply in the moonlight. Edith examined the metallic instruments of torture and smiled. 'A woman after my own heart,' she beamed. Then she saw what she was looking for.

Stacked in the corner of the room were crates of the head-lice shampoo Mr Tick had bulk-bought earlier that day from the local market.

Grabbing a bottle and unscrewing the top, she sniffed at the stinking liquid inside.

'Sooo, Aggie Malkin,' she grinned, as she poured the shampoo down the sink and dipped the empty bottle into her bag to refill it, 'you think you're the only one who can mix together a magic potion, do you? Well, once the pupils wash their hair in *my* concoction, the fun will *really* start!'

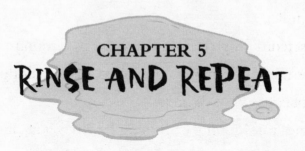

CHAPTER 5
RINSE AND REPEAT

James, Lenny and Alexander stood at the doorway to the school hall and stared ahead in amazement at the snaking queue of pupils lining up to have their heads examined by Granny Tick on the stage.

'It's worse than yesterday!' exclaimed James.

Alexander nodded. 'Years ten and eleven are involved now. Apparently Gordon's been bullying them, too, so they all have to be checked.'

'Your nan looks like she's holding court up there,' said Lenny, as he munched his way through a cheese and pickle sandwich.

'My dad moved her in here because the screams were putting him off his solitaire games,' explained Alexander.

A scream erupted from the stage as Granny Tick's metal comb battled against a particularly complicated knot of hair.

James ran his fingers through his own hair and winced at the memories of yesterday. 'Did you wash your hair in that stuff last night?' he asked.

'Is the atomic weight of titanium sixty-three point four?' replied Alexander.

James and Lenny simply stared at him.

The headmaster's son sighed. 'No, it isn't, and no, I didn't!' he clarified. 'That shampoo smells worse than the caretaker's socks!'

James and Lenny turned their silent attention back to the queue for the stage, the larger boy taking another bite out of his sandwich. Alexander hopped from foot to foot for a moment, then burst out: 'In case you're wondering, the *real* atomic weight of titanium is forty-seven point eight six seven!'

James checked his watch. 'Twelve seconds,' he announced.

'I wondered how long it would take him,' said Lenny through a mouthful of cheddar.

'Very funny,' snapped Alexander, 'but if we're ever in an exam and –' His sentence was cut short as the hall doors crashed open and two year-ten girls burst out.

'There is no way on *earth* I'm washing my hair in this stuff!' one of them screamed, slamming the bottle down on to a nearby chair. A thick, green foam oozed from the top of the bottle and splashed on to the seat, fizzing as it made contact with the thin material.

As the girls headed into the toilets, James made his way over to the chair. 'What colour was the shampoo in the bottle you were given yesterday?' he asked.

'Purple,' said Alexander. 'Why?'

'Mine too,' said James, carefully picking up the bottle and examining it. 'This looks wrong.' He sniffed at the contents and quickly pulled his face away in disgust. 'It smells wrong, too!'

Without waiting to be invited, he pushed the bottle under Lenny's nose and watched as his friend's eyes began to water. Sprinting over to the nearest bin, Lenny spat out his latest mouthful of sandwich. 'I'm going to stop hanging round with you two,' he moaned, as he dropped the remainder of his lunch into the bin.

'This shampoo's different from the stuff your granny was giving out yesterday,' said James, looking from Alexander to Lenny and back again. The boys sighed.

'Here he goes,' moaned Alexander. 'Claiming something spooky is up. It could just be a different batch.'

'Your dad bought it in bulk from some bloke on the market who makes his own cosmetics in the kitchen sink,' said James. 'I doubt he ever made more than a bathful of the nit shampoo.' He sniffed at the contents of the bottle again. 'Whatever *this* is, it's not for cleaning hair.'

'So?' said Lenny. 'What do we do?'

'We take this to the science lab and have Einstein here find out what's in it,' said James, gesturing to Alexander.

The headmaster's son held up his hands in protest. 'And what makes you think I want to give up my lunch hour to muck about with chemicals in the science lab?' he asked.

'Because that's what you do every other day of the week,' answered James.

'He's got a point,' agreed Lenny.

'Come on,' said James. 'If someone has swapped the nit shampoo for something harmful, your nan could get the blame – and you don't want to be responsible for letting that happen to a sweet, frail old lady, do you?'

'Sweet, frail old lady?' exclaimed Alexander. 'Are we talking about the same woman who you claimed had left grooves in your scalp yesterday?'

'It doesn't mean I want to see her arrested!' countered James.

Alexander's shoulders sagged. 'All right,' he said, pulling a key from his pocket. 'This way.' He set off.

'How come he has his own key to the science lab?' Lenny wondered, staring after him.

Alexander peered through the microscope at the teeming micro-organisms that filled the Petri dish.

'It's like nothing I've ever seen before!' he said, concerned. Raising his head, he gestured for James to take his place. 'Have a look.'

James hesitated. 'What's the point of me having a look?' he asked. 'I'm so good at chemistry I set fire to my tie with a Bunsen burner in the last exam. There's no way I'd know what I was looking at!'

'I think you'll be interested in this,' said Alexander, stepping aside.

James peered through the eyepiece of the microscope for a second before looking up, his face pale.

'They look like little ghosts,' he said.

'*Exactly*,' replied Alexander. 'And there's only one place bacteria like that could come from.'

'The plague pit,' said James, smugly.

'Is it harmful?' asked Lenny, ignoring James's look of self-satisfaction.

49

'Possibly,' replied Alexander. 'But without one of us using it and examining the results, I couldn't tell you exactly how.'

'So there's no way you can put together an antidote?' said James. 'Something to cancel out its effects?'

'Not unless you want to start showering under laboratory conditions,' said Alexander. The boys mulled this over for a moment before Alexander's face lit up. He grabbed a clipboard and pen. 'We could go to the showers in the sports hall and –'

'No way!' interrupted James. 'Ghostly shampoo or no ghostly shampoo, I'm not becoming your scientific guinea pig for anything!'

'Then there's only one way to find out what this stuff does,' said Alexander, lowering his eyes back to the microscope.

James and Lenny exchanged a glance, knowing what was coming next.

'We wait.'

CHAPTER 6
REDKING212

Mr Tick slid the arrow across the screen, dropping a red ace on to the black two and watching with satisfaction as the computer-generated cards began to bounce around the screen. Another Internet Team Solitaire match won. Whoever Solitguy really was, he'd think twice about challenging RedKing212 again.

Standing, Mr Tick took a moment to gaze around his office. Since moving his mother's nit search to the school hall, his office was once again a peaceful haven away from the hustle and bustle of the rest of the building.

A 'ding' from the computer made Mr Tick glance back at the screen. A message was flashing: 'Play again RedKing212?'

The headmaster laughed. Sorry Solitguy, one defeat at the hands of Grimesford's solitaire master would have to be enough for one day. Mind you . . . it would be something to talk about in the solitaire chat room he visited each evening, Solitaire's Not Just For Saddos.

Curling the edges of his mouth up into a smile that Mr Tick was convinced made him look like a sly secret agent, he reached over and clicked the 'yes' button. 'So, Solitguy,' he said in his smoothest voice, 'we meet again, and this time – it's personal!'

As Solitguy dragged a black seven over to an available red eight, Mr Tick glanced up at the mirror on the wall to check that his secret-agent smile was still in place.

That's when he noticed the hair sticking up.

Leaping to his feet, the headmaster grabbed his novelty playing-card-shaped comb and attempted to brush the unruly lock into place. It sprang back to attention immediately and waggled about, as if daring him to try and control it.

A 'beep' from the computer announced that Solitguy had completed his first suit of cards and was well on the way to winning the game. Mr Tick grunted and tried again to smooth back down his animated clump of hair.

The lock jumped straight back up and the headmaster leant closer to the mirror to inspect it. Something was moving about in his hair . . .

A nit!

With a scream that would have made a four-year-old girl proud, Mr Tick jumped on to his office chair and repeatedly slapped his head. 'Lice! Lice!' he squealed, twisting round on his chair and falling on to his desk.

As he fumbled around for his dropped comb, he accidentally clicked the 'resign' icon on the screen, immediately losing to Solitguy.

The nit leapt from his hair and landed on the end of Mr Tick's nose, giving the headmaster what he decided was definitely an evil, menacing look.

Reaching out, Mr Tick grabbed a heavy dictionary from a nearby shelf and began to hit

himself in the face with it. 'Get it off me!' he cried.

The office door opened.

When Miss Keys described the scene later in the staff room over a cup of tea, she blamed Mr Tick's outburst on stress. However, as she stood in the doorway, open-mouthed, she was convinced that the headmaster had gone insane.

'Mr Tick?' she asked, nervously. 'Are you OK?'

The headmaster flipped over on his desk, jamming a pencil up his nose and scanning the room for the monster nit that had attacked him.

'I'm fine, Miss Keys!' he assured his secretary as he clambered to his feet and attempted to smooth down the tangled mess of his hair. 'However, I'm afraid that the head-lice shampoo I purchased yesterday doesn't appear to have worked. Could you get me the managing director of the manufacturer on the phone?'

'Managing director?' asked Miss Keys, bending to pick up the dictionary and place it back on its shelf. 'There isn't one, sir. All we have is the mobile number for Big Dave on the market stall.'

'Of course,' said Mr Tick, nodding.

'Will there be anything else?' said Miss Keys.

'No, no. You run along and get yourself a sandwich. I'll be fine,' beamed the headmaster, straightening his tie and closing the solitaire program on his computer, the flashing 'You lose RedKing212 – Solitguy wins!' message not helping his mood.

'If you're sure,' said Miss Keys, closing the office door and heading back to her own desk.

The headmaster sat quietly in his chair for a second, breathing calmly and trying to regain his composure. The intercom buzzed.

'Yes, Miss Keys?' said Mr Tick, pressing the red button.

His secretary was staring at him through the tiny glass window in the office door. 'You still have a pencil up your nose, sir,' she told him.

Miss Keys picked her way along the corridor towards the canteen, a sandwich being the last thing on her mind. First the headmaster's moment of madness, and now this.

There were groups of pupils everywhere, scratching furiously at their scalps and crying. Some of them had blood-stained fingers where they'd scratched too hard, while others were attacking their hair with scissors to try and rid themselves of the nits which continued to drive them crazy.

'This isn't right,' the secretary said to herself, as she crossed the playground and pushed open the canteen doors. Chaos reigned. Pupils writhed about on tables, pouring bottles of water over their heads in an effort to cool the burning bites of the head lice. 'This isn't right at all!'

Turning, Miss Keys raced back to her office, leaping over screaming pupils with blood dripping from their scalps. Breaking the habit of a lifetime, she flung Mr Tick's door open without knocking and dashed inside.

'Well, you make sure that it's here by first thing tomorrow!' roared the headmaster, slamming the telephone receiver down. 'Great news, Miss Keys!' he grinned. 'Big Dave has agreed to replace the shampoo I bought with a batch of extra-strength lotion free of charge!'

'I think we'll need it, sir,' replied his secretary. 'We've got a problem!'

Unseen by the sobbing pupils, Edith Codd danced her way along the school corridor. She'd done it, even if she wasn't exactly certain how.

Whatever mixture she had put together, it had

turned ordinary head lice into a plague of flesh-eating zombie nits. Her little army was hard at work, biting through the scalps of the infected.

A year-ten girl screamed as she pulled her hands away from her hair to find them covered in blood. The nits were starting to bite the fingertips that scratched them as well as the children's scalps.

Edith clapped her hands together and skipped through the wall into the girls' toilets to find pupils pushing their heads into toilet bowls and flushing water over their hair.

'I'll be remembered for this!' Edith sang to herself. 'Once the zombie nits get a taste for flesh, they'll move on to other parts of the body and soon the school will be littered with the skeletons of its pupils, picked clean by my lovely lice!'

A year-eight girl ran through her to the get to the mirror above the sinks, squealing in terror as she watched lines of crimson blood dripping down her forehead. She reached up and began to rip her hair out of her scalp in clumps. Edith's head swum with happiness.

'Oh, yes,' she said. 'I'll be remembered for this!'

CHAPTER 7
RAT PACK

'I'll never forget you did this!' roared William
Scroggins, as he stomped about the amphitheatre.
Hundreds of ghosts looked on as his words caused
Edith to beam with delight.

'I *knew* you'd be pleased!' she said.

The ghostly audience nodded their approval.

'*Pleased?*' demanded William. 'How can I be
pleased when children – my friends – are in pain?'

The watching spirits instantly swapped sides
and tutted disapproval for Edith's actions.

'Your *friends?*' scoffed Edith. 'Just because you

go up there and eavesdrop on their conversations doesn't make them your friends! The pupils of St Sebastian's have disturbed us too many times, and they're getting what they deserve!'

A reluctant smattering of applause echoed around the auditorium.

'If you wanted them to be quiet, there are kinder ways of doing it!' bellowed William. The applause quickly died out. 'You've created a plague of zombie nits!'

Edith grinned. 'Aren't they wonderful?'

By now, the ghosts were too confused to pick one side over the other, so they resigned themselves to sitting quietly until the argument was over.

'No, they are *not* wonderful!' shouted William. 'They're *hurting* people! Ambrose and I demand that you call them off.'

The older spirit who, until this moment, had been leaning back against Edith's upturned barrel minding his own business, began to choke on the leech in his mouth. 'Don't drag me into this!' he spluttered.

'You see?' snapped Edith, gesturing to Ambrose Harbottle as he reached an ectoplasmic hand down his throat and extracted the leech. 'No one cares what you think, little boy! Now, run away and play in the sewers!'

Before William could reply, Edith reached into a pile of bones at her feet and extracted a skull. She banged it on the barrel and shouted, 'Meeting suspended!'

From the back of the audience, a tiny voice shouted, 'Hey! That's mine!'

As hundreds of ghosts filed thankfully out of the amphitheatre, William sank to the ground and sighed. Ambrose patted him on the back as he passed. 'I didn't mean . . . That is, I didn't think that she . . .'

'It's OK, Ambrose,' said William, smiling up at the older ghost. 'I know.' Before long, he was alone.

He sat in silence for a few moments, feeling helpless. Then, taking a deep breath, he stood and began to make his way towards the sewer tunnels.

A noise startled him and he turned to see another ghost, Bertram Ruttle, approaching. He had a bone with holes drilled into it pressed to his lips and he was playing it like a flute.

'You OK?' asked Bertram, pausing the tune.

'I've been better,' replied William.

'I've been working on something,' said Bertram. 'Thought it might cheer you up.' He raised the flute to his mouth again and began to play an uptempo jig.

Nothing happened for a moment, but then William became aware of the patter of thousands of pairs of feet. Suddenly, hordes of rats swarmed out of the sewer tunnels and filled the amphitheatre.

William watched, stunned, as the rats lined up behind Bertram and began to follow him as he danced around the cavern, playing his jig.

'How are you doing that?' the young ghost asked.

'Doing what?' said Bertram.

As soon as he stopped playing, the rats began to race for the exits. With a wink, Bertram blew into the bone flute again and the rats instantly scurried back into line and began to follow the ghostly musician once more.

'Could I try that?' asked William, the beginnings of an idea starting to form in his mind.

'No problem,' said Bertram, handing over the flute. As soon as he stopped playing, the rats made another dash for the sewer pipes.

William raised the flute to his lips and blew as the last of the rats left the amphitheatre.

At first, no sound came out but, after a few moments of trying, he managed a small squeak. To his amazement, one pink nose appeared from a hole in the wall.

'Gently does it,' coaxed Bertram, as William blew into the flute again.

This time, the note was longer, and several pairs of eyes appeared from around the cavern.

Before long, William managed to pick out a simple melody.

One by one, the rats emerged from the darkness. Cautiously at first, they began to edge their way across the open space towards the young ghost.

William tried not to grin as the rodents crept ever closer. Concentrating hard, he began his tune again, picking up speed and tapping his foot in time to the music.

Rats began to pour from the sewer pipes, tumbling towards William in their hundreds. The little, pale ghost skipped around the amphitheatre, marvelling at the tide of rodents that followed his every move.

Bertram Ruttle reached behind Edith's podium and grabbed a pair of leg bones. He began to

beat out a rhythm on the upturned barrel to accompany William's flute playing.

Soon, the rats were dancing around the cavern, their whiskers twitching in time to the music that had bewitched them.

William splashed from puddle to puddle, the flute high in the air as his plan to rid St Sebastian's of the zombie nits came closer to reality.

Finally exhausted, the ghosts stopped playing and watched as the swarm of rats realised that the spell had been broken and scattered away into the darkness.

'Do you think I could –' began William, but Bertram held up a hand to silence him.

'Already ahead of you!' smiled the musician as he produced another bone flute, this one much smaller.

William took it and began to blow his tune. The sound was shriller – higher pitched. No rats appeared.

'It's not working,' he said.

'Maybe not for rats . . .' said Bertram, winking.

William gripped the bone flute in his hand and raced for the sewer pipe that led up to the boys' toilets.

Edith appeared in the amphitheatre and glared at him.

'Don't you dare!' she warned.

William raised the flute to his lips and blew a little toot as he ran straight through Edith and into the darkness beyond.

'William Scroggins!' screamed Edith. 'Get back here!'

CHAPTER 8
HAT'S THE WAY TO DO IT

James leant back against the wall of the bike sheds and tried once again to improve Alexander's mood. 'Don't be so hard on yourself,' he said.

'What other choice do I have?' moaned Alexander. 'I can't figure out what's in that fake shampoo!'

'It's not your fault everyone's scratching like mad,' said Lenny.

'I know that,' exclaimed Alexander. 'I'm more concerned that I've hit a science problem I can't find a solution to!'

James and Lenny exchanged glances.

'And here we were thinking you were concerned for the well-being of your fellow pupils,' said James.

Alexander didn't reply.

'Right,' said James. 'Let's not dwell on what we don't know – let's focus on the facts. One: the school has been hit by an infestation of lice.'

'Brought here by Gordon Carver,' added Lenny.

James nodded. 'Two: the plague-pit ghosts replaced the head-lice shampoo with something that seems to have transformed the lice into a horde of zombie nits.'

'That even Nitty Nora can't control,' Lenny chipped in.

James shuddered at the thought. 'Three,' he said, 'everyone infected with the zombie nits has started scratching themselves so hard that they draw blood.'

'You're the science guy, Alexander,' said Lenny. 'What can we do?'

Alexander shrugged. 'We could wear hats,' he suggested.

'*Hats*?' said James. 'That's your scientific solution to this? We wear hats?'

'I've told you, I don't *have* a scientific solution,' moaned the headmaster's son. 'The lice appear to be too small to actually turn their hosts into zombies and, if the rest of us who aren't infected wear hats, it should stop the spread of the lice around the school.'

'I told you he could do it,' grinned James. Lenny nodded in agreement.

'Do what?' asked Alexander.

'Think of a way to help until we can stop the attack,' replied James.

Alexander began to smile. 'I suppose it is pretty good advice,' he said. 'And I know the best place in school to find hats. Follow me!' He leapt to his feet and marched off in the direction of the school hall.

James turned to Lenny as they followed. 'Next time it's your turn to massage his ego,' he said.

'Hats! Get your hats here!' shouted Alexander, as the three boys wandered away from the drama room handing out whatever protective headgear they could find.

James adjusted the brim of his cowboy hat and glanced around. 'I hope we don't bump into Stacey,' he said, referring to the one girl in school who could always make him blush.

'Why?' asked Lenny, untying the string that held the earflaps of his deerstalker in place. 'She might be impressed with a rough, tough cowpoke like yourself!'

James ignored the jibe and gestured towards

Alexander, who was busy explaining to a group of year-nine pupils that the hats would protect them from the zombie nits. 'Why do you think he chose the rainbow clown wig instead of a hat?'

Lenny pulled a pipe he had found in the props room out of his pocket and sucked on the end, Sherlock Holmes style. 'I don't know,' he said. 'Maybe it brings out the colour of his eyes.'

After handing out an assortment of gladiator helmets, bonnets and headscarves, the classrooms were soon filled with both teachers and pupils wearing varied headgear. Anyone infected by the zombie nits was forced to sit out on the sports field, where the sight of their itching didn't put everyone else off their lessons.

Before long, the scratching pupils had started to help out by combing through each other's hair, and picking out the offending nits.

'It's just like a nature documentary I saw about chimpanzees,' said Lenny as they handed out the final hat – a town-crier's tricorne – to Mr Downe.

The religious studies teacher leant in to Alexander and hissed: 'Don't tell your granny that you've seen me!' Then he rammed the hat hard on to his head and trotted away down the corridor, his eyes darting from side to side.

With everyone either protected or infected, the boys were setting off for their own classroom when they found themselves faced with Mr Tick.

The headmaster stopped and stared at their headgear but, before any of them could explain why they were out of class and apparently in fancy dress, he gestured for the trio to follow him.

'The delivery of extra-strength lotion has arrived,' he explained. 'Help me unload it from the van.'

Mr Tick led James, Alexander and Lenny out into the playground, where a battered white van was waiting with its rear doors open. Dozens of plain cardboard boxes filled with yellow bottles sat inside.

'Are you sure this stuff is safe?' asked Alexander, as he rummaged through the first of the boxes. The bottles appeared to have had their original labels torn off and the contents – extra-strength nit lotion – written on in marker pen. The word 'lotion' was spelt 'loshun'.

'It had better be,' replied Mr Tick. 'I had to tip Big Dave thirty pounds not to dump it all at the school gates when a police car went past.'

The boys set about carrying box after box of the lotion into Mr Tick's office, where Miss Keys was busy pouring what remained of the ghostly shampoo down the drain.

It hissed as it hit the sink and a cloud of green vapour surrounded the school secretary as she worked.

'Well, at least we've seen the end of that stuff,' said James.

'Let's just hope this lotion does the job,' added Lenny.

'Right,' said Mr Tick, stopping to examine his hair in the mirror for the fifteenth time that hour. 'You boys can head back to your classroom now.'

77

'Don't you want us to distribute the nit lotion?' asked Alexander.

'No,' came the reply. 'I'll be keeping that here for the time being. I don't want to hand it out until I've, er, had a chance to test it out myself.' The headmaster paused to check his hair in the mirror again.

'You won't need the lotion as long as you protect yourself with some sort of hat,' explained Alexander.

'Is that so?' said Mr Tick, plucking the wig from his son's head and pulling it on to his own.

'Hey!' yelled Alexander, yanking the back of his school jumper up to cover his bare head. 'That's my wig!'

'Then consider it confiscated!' snapped the headmaster, as he closed the door on the boys. Turning, he noticed Miss Keys smiling at him from his private bathroom.

'Is there something wrong, Miss Keys?' he asked.

'Oh, no, headmaster,' breathed the secretary. 'It's just that I've never seen you with such a full head of hair before!'

'I used to have quite the style in my younger days,' said Mr Tick, fluffing up the edges of the nylon clown wig. 'Nothing too dramatic, but a reasonable-sized quiff, always well oiled.'

'I'm sure you looked very handsome, sir,' said Miss Keys as she edged towards her handbag on the chair near the door.

The headmaster examined his reflection in the mirror, trying out his secret-agent smile with this new multicoloured hairdo.

'Yes,' he said, almost to himself. 'I suppose I was.'

There was a small click and a flash but, when Mr Tick spun round, his secretary was standing with her hands behind her back, an innocent smile creeping across her face.

That one, thought Miss Keys to herself, *is going on the front page of the web site!*

CHAPTER 9
HOP TO IT

Mr Downe locked the cubicle door and sighed. At last, the one place where Granny Tick and her nasty nit combs couldn't find him: the boys' toilets.

He had deliberately avoided the staff toilets because going there would have meant passing the doors of the school hall where the wicked old woman still had her stall of pain set up. No, this was the place to be – quiet, safe and free of torture. He could finally relax.

The teacher leant back against the cubicle door and took a deep breath. Ahhh! It felt good to be free of the – what was *that*? Mr Downe watched in horror as the water in the toilet began to bubble and hiss, his face turning a pale green colour in the process.

He gripped his briefcase and pushed himself back against the cubicle wall as a hand burst out of the water; a hand clutching a small bone with holes drilled through it. The teacher screamed.

Mr Downe scrabbled for the lock on the door, his fingers fumbling with the tiny bolt. He pounded at the wood with his fists, begging to be freed as an arm followed the hand out of the toilet bowl and the top of a head appeared.

Throwing his briefcase over the partition, Mr Downe scrambled up its sides and threw himself over, too, landing heavily on the floor.

With a barely contained sob, she raced through the door and away from whatever monster Granny Tick had conjured up to haunt him.

By the time William stepped through the door of the cubicle, the toilets were deserted. The only evidence that Mr Downe had been there at all was the crushed tricorne hat on the spot where he had hit the ground.

William stepped carefully along the corridor towards Mr Tick's office. The nit-free pupils were all busy in class. Out on the sports field, Mr Thomas, the drama teacher – the only staff member brave enough to be near the infected children – was shouting maths problems through a megaphone to the itchy victims, a bald cap pulled firmly down over his head to protect his own hair.

Behind the young ghost, Edith Codd floated, invisible to all.

'Where are you going with that flute, my pretty?' she hissed to herself, as William reached the headmaster's office and paused to listen at the door. 'Whatever you think you're up to, William Scroggins,' she muttered, 'I'll be watching you!'

Mr Tick finished his email to Solitguy explaining that a computer malfunction had made their latest solitaire match null and void and that he was still in the lead by three games to nil.

Hitting the 'send' button, he glanced up at the mirror on the wall and realised that he was still wearing the clown wig. 'Time to see what this extra-strength nit lotion can do,' he said, pulling the rainbow-coloured hairpiece from his head.

Checking that Miss Keys was busy, Mr Tick grabbed a bottle of the lotion from the pile of boxes and sniffed cautiously at the lid. It certainly smelt better than the shampoo.

Unscrewing the top, he raised the bottle of yellow fluid to his hairline and tipped it forwards.

At that moment William, unable to hear any noise inside the office, made the mistake of sliding his head through the door to see if anyone was there. Forgetting to become invisible, he found himself staring into the terrified eyes of

Mr Tick, a drop of thick lotion leaving the bottle and heading for his fringe.

The fright made the headmaster jump backwards and drop the bottle on the floor, where upon its contents spurted out all over his Italian leather shoes.

There was a hiss and a burning smell. Mr Tick gazed down in horror to see the leather of his shoes melting away as the yellow fluid ate through it.

Quickly, he kicked the shoes off his feet and flung them into the corner, where the lotion continued to eat away at the leather. 'Thank goodness that stuff never touched my head!' said the headmaster aloud, stepping over a small pool of it that was fizzing on the carpet.

Reaching out tentatively, he rubbed the spot on the door where the boy's face had appeared. It was solid wood.

I'm losing it, thought Mr Tick as he padded round the desk and slumped into his chair. *This day just can't get any worse.*

With a 'ding' an email arrived from Solitguy threatening to report RedKing212 to the British Solitaire Society if he didn't admit he'd lost their last game.

Mr Tick kicked the leg of his desk in frustration, remembering that he was only wearing socks just a split-second too late.

William Scroggins pulled his head out of the office door and was turning to run when he saw Edith standing at the far end of the corridor. She didn't look happy.

I'm trapped! thought the young ghost. *I can't go down there or Edith will drag me back to the sewer. And I've just scared the life out of Mr Tick!*

Edith began to walk towards him, a dark expression on her face.

William had to think fast. 'Well,' he said to himself, 'everyone says I look a lot like Alexander Tick. Now's the time to put it to the test!'

Concentrating hard, William turned himself solid, grabbed the handle of the door to Miss

Keys's office and stepped inside.

'I've come to see my father, Mr Tick!' he declared, doing his best Alexander impression. He was pleased that his insides had decomposed long ago or they would have been churning around.

Miss Keys glanced up from the letter she was writing and shook her head. 'He's busy at the moment. He told me not to let anyone in until he said it was OK.'

Edith appeared in the doorway behind William, invisible to Miss Keys but very much visible to the terrified young ghost. She reached out a hand to grab him.

'Do you know who I am?' he demanded. 'I am the real Alexander Tick, and I demand to see my real father, the real headmaster, Richard Tick!'

Miss Keys sighed. 'Alexander, I will not let you disturb the headmaster,' she said. 'He could be in the middle of an important phone call, or dealing with sensitive financial matters.'

She glanced through the small window in the connecting door to see Mr Tick hopping round his office, clutching at his toe.

Edith was in the office now, her hand around William's neck. The young ghost had to act.

'This is a matter of life or, er, a death that won't be worth living,' he shouted, glancing back at Edith.

Wriggling free of her grip, he pushed open the door to Mr Tick's office and bellowed: 'Father! I am your son, Alexander Tick!'

Both Edith and Miss Keys glared at the door as it swung shut behind him.

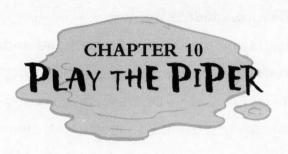

CHAPTER 10
PLAY THE PIPER

'What are you doing here?' groaned Mr Tick, as he flopped back into his chair and pulled off his sock to massage his aching toe.

William glanced back at Edith in Miss Keys's office. The school secretary stood beside the ghost, completely unaware that she was there.

'I've come to see you, my father, headmaster Richard Tick!' said William, his voice trembling. He wasn't sure this was going to work.

Luckily, Mr Tick didn't pay William much attention, aside from looking at his medieval rags and commenting: 'I suppose you're in this school play I've not been told about as well, are you?'

He began to write a strongly worded reply to Solitguy's email and, for a moment, seemed to forget that William was even there.

The ghost stayed silent and concentrated on remaining solid. He tried not to think about how strange a situation this was. Neither he nor Mr Tick knew that, elsewhere in the school, things were starting to get even stranger.

Out on the sports field, Mr Thomas pulled his coat closed against the biting wind and yelled through the megaphone: 'If x equals nine and y equals seven, what is the square root of x plus y?'

The head lice-infected pupils struggled to keep their exercise books open and write down their answers until the zombie nits suddenly began to jump from their scalps and on to the grass.

The pupils watched in amazement as legions of the tiny insects marched as one towards the main building. Relieved that the vicious creatures had left their hair, they began to cheer loudly.

Mr Thomas jumped out of the nits' way as they swarmed across the sports field and piled up against the back entrance to the school. The sheer weight of them was enough to force down the door handles and pull open the doors, and they spilt inside . . .

At the sound of the cheering from the sports field, Mr Tick looked up from his email. He noticed that William was still there.

'What is it you want, Alexander?' he asked.

William panicked slightly. His disguise was working – Mr Tick believed that he was his son – but now he had to come up with a reason for being in the office. He quickly settled on what remained of the headmaster's shoes.

'It's your shoes, Father. I –'

But William didn't get to finish the rest of

the sentence because, at that moment, the office
door crashed open and what appeared to be a
seething black carpet swarmed into the room.

Mr Tick belted out his best four-year-old girl
squeal again and leapt up on to the desk.

The zombie nits, however, weren't interested in
him. They made straight for the shoes – or, to be
more exact – the extra-strength nit lotion that
had eaten away at his shoes.

The nits rolled around in it, swam in it, and drank it. If you'd been able to get in close, you'd have heard tiny shouts of 'Geronimo!' as they jumped off each others' shoulders into the lotion and did the backstroke.

All the while, Mr Tick was standing on his desk, throwing items of stationery at them: pens, pencils, paper clips – anything he could get his hands on.

He soon stopped his attack when a handful of the nits took offence and threw a pencil back at him, scoring a bullseye and wedging it back up his nose.

William stared at the bone flute in his hand and a sense of power overwhelmed him. He hadn't even started to play the thing and, already, the zombie nits had come to him. Here was his chance to rid the school of the infestation for good!

Raising the flute to his lips, he splashed into the puddle of nit lotion and started to pick out his simple tune.

The zombie nits stopped swimming for a second and all turned to look up at him. There was something different about this boy. He didn't appear to have any blood in his system to feed on, for a start. Still, the nits couldn't complain. The only thing this party had been missing was some music, and now the boy was playing some.

William began to dance his way out of the office, his feet sticky and slippery with the extra-strength nit lotion. The nits watched the source of all their happiness trailing out of the office and gave chase.

William glanced behind, delighted to see that his tune was working. The zombie nits were following him!

He began to dance as he played, revealing the soles of his shoes more, which gave the zombie nits something to chase. They swarmed after him, along the corridor, in pursuit of the lotion.

Miss Keys and a still-invisible Edith stood in

the doorway to the secretary's office watching as William danced away with what appeared to be a black cloak dragging behind him.

'Oh, no, you don't, Scroggins!' sneered Edith, as she turned and ran through the wall into Mr Tick's private bathroom.

With a splash, she dived head first into the toilet and slithered her way past the U-bend, aiming to reach the sewers before William had a chance to get there with his crowd of insect followers.

Mr Tick waited, crouched on his desk, the pencil still jammed up his nose, until he was certain that the zombie nits weren't coming back.

Then, slowly, he climbed down off the desk and peered into the corner where the scraps of leather that had once been his finest Italian shoes now lay on the carpet. The extra-strength lotion had been completely slurped up by the zombie nits.

Cautiously, he reached down and picked up

one of the scraps of black leather and examined it. What was it about the shoes that had caused them to dissolve so quickly? He ought to find out before he pulled his replacement pair from the desk drawer and put them on.

He turned the leather over in his hands, looking for clues, but didn't find any. Raising the material to his nose, he inhaled deeply and breathed in what was now a mixture of foot sweat, head-lice lotion and zombie-nit droppings.

Mr Tick's face screwed up as the odour invaded his senses. It seemed to burn into his brain and made his eyes want to leave his head for a while until everything calmed down again.

Finally, Mr Tick sneezed, launching the pencil out of his nose and impaling it in the toe he had recently stubbed on the leg of his desk.

He would never know that Miss Keys had been quick enough to record the sound of his scream for her new web site.

CHAPTER 11
BATTLE OF THE BANDS

'No, no, no!' yelled Bertram Ruttle, as the Plague
Pit Junior Ghost Band played yet another series
of wrong notes in their rendition of Bertram's
self-penned tune, 'Edith Is A Loony'.

'Wait until the chorus have sung the line
"Hold your breath cos here she comes again!"
before beginning the middle eight section,' he
announced to the ghosts of children who sat
facing him, each clutching an instrument made
from the bones of those buried in the pit. 'Now,
once more from the start.'

A mess of sounds echoed around the amphitheatre as drums, trumpets, whistles and bagpipes attempted to play the same song at the same time.

'She's got a face like the back end of a donkey,' sang the rest of the children who made up the choir.

Bertram smiled. The plague-pit ghosts would love this when the band played it for the annual Great Fire of Grimesford party the spirits held each year. Of course, Edith may not be too impressed, but he really didn't care.

The choir had just sung, 'Her body's like a wet sack of potatoes' when the star of the song raced out of one of the sewer pipes.

The children stopped singing and playing as soon as they saw Edith, but Bertram, who had his back to the sewer entrance, hadn't noticed her arrival.

'Why have you stopped?' he demanded. 'We

were just getting to the line "Her hairstyle looks like a badger's bum"!'

Edith's face filled his vision as she leapt in front of him.

'*What* did you say?' she demanded.

Bertram looked horrified, and several of the young ghosts began to cry.

'I, er, said that your hair is so wonderful that it makes me want to *hum* . . .' lied Bertram, desperately.

'Oh?' said the old hag, puzzled.

'Yes, y-y-you know,' stuttered Bertram, 'erm . . . hum an ode – to your beauty.'

'Well, that's all right then,' oozed Edith, twirling a lock of her fuzzy red hair and grimacing. Bertram winced at the sight of her foul teeth.

From the back of the band, the youngest musician – who played a shaker made from a kneecap filled with dried rat droppings – spoke up. 'Is that her?' he asked.

The other children shushed him, but he continued his quest for knowledge. 'Is that the one who looks like the back end of a donkey?'

Edith turned on the children and snarled at them, her teeth like broken headstones jutting from a rotting graveyard. Maggots and ticks swarmed over her tongue. The children screamed.

'I need an instrument!' roared Edith, reaching out and trying to pull a leg-bone trombone from a young girl's hands.

'Leave her alone!' demanded Bertram, grabbing hold of the other end of the trombone and pulling in the opposite direction.

'Her hairstyle really *is* like a badger's bum!' announced the boy from the back of the band.

Edith screamed and released her grip on the trombone, causing Bertram and the girl to tumble back in the dirt of the amphitheatre floor.

Spotting a bone guitar with stretched leeches for strings in the hands of another junior musician, the old woman lunged for it.

'Give me that!' she yelled.

But the owner of the guitar – a mop-haired youth with a liking for death-metal music – wouldn't give up his instrument.

'George!' shouted Bertram. 'Don't let her take it from you!' The ghostly music teacher launched himself on to Edith's back and forced the old crone face down into the dirt.

George snatched his precious guitar away from the feuding adults and checked it for damage.

Bertram pulled his bone flute out of his pocket and began to beat Edith across the head with it. The older ghost pulled her face out of the muck and found the small boy with the shaker sitting cross-legged directly in front of her.

'Yep,' he announced calmly to his friends. 'She's definitely a loony.'

A crowd had gathered to watch William dance along the corridor playing his flute, hordes of zombie nits trailing after him. Pupils and teachers watched from classroom doors and windows, applauding loudly at the sight of what they believed was Alexander leading the insects away.

As he passed the door to the girls' toilets, it burst open and a very angry Edith appeared, a stolen bone xylophone strapped to her chest. She hadn't even stopped when, as she'd raced along the sewer pipes, a voice had recognised the bones and cried out: 'Hey, they're mine!'

Edith began to beat at the xylophone noisily, trying to drown out William's flute and lead the zombie nits away from him.

What neither she nor William knew, however, was that the lice were chasing the extra-strength nit lotion that still clung to the soles of William's shoes. The wonderful music was just an added bonus to them.

The bell rang to signal the end of the period and added to the horrible confusion of sounds in the corridor.

William began to blow harder into his flute, prompting Edith to beat even more furiously at the xylophone.

The watching pupils and teachers jammed their hands over their ears as the noise became unbearable.

Edith hammered at the bones strapped in front of her so hard that, with a sickening crack, the xylophone shattered and fell to the floor.

She screamed as she tried to scoop up what remained of the instrument and then, with a last sneer at the triumphant William, she melted back through the wall of the toilets and disappeared.

Suddenly, Mr Tick appeared beside the young ghost, blood trailing from his injured toe as he limped along next to what he still believed was his son.

'Well done, Alexander!' he shouted, attempting to dance along to the music.

From the doorway of their classroom, James, Lenny and the real Alexander watched in amazement.

'I think your dad's having some sort of fit,' marvelled Lenny.

'No,' said Alexander. 'He's dancing. I saw him do it once at my Aunt Claire's wedding. It was a good three songs before people realised he hadn't electrocuted himself on the sound system.'

'Never mind that, Stick,' said James, pointing to William. 'What are *you* doing out there playing that flute?'

'I don't know,' said Alexander flatly, as he stared at the double of himself dancing along the corridor, 'but I appear to be very good at it.'

At the head of the zombie-nit parade, William spun round as he played and earnt a round of applause from the watching crowds.

Mr Tick, caught up in the moment, also attempted to spin round but he slipped in the blood that was still pouring from his toe and fell face first into a year-nine girl's schoolbag.

When he re-emerged, he had another pencil jammed firmly up his nose.

CHAPTER 12
THEY THINK IT'S ALL OVER . . .

The following morning, the entire school gathered
in the hall for a special assembly. Most of the
pupils and teachers – both those who hadn't been
affected and those who had suffered at the hands
of the zombie nits – were still wearing either a hat
or a wig for protection, just in case.

Mr Tick climbed on to the stage and gazed
out over a sea of witches, policemen and soldiers.
Beside him sat Granny Tick, a plaited wig pulled
down over her ears. She looked like a dumpy,
sour-faced milkmaid.

Mr Drew, the music teacher, played a few bars
of an old Elvis Presley song – 'From A Jack To
A King' – the theme tune Mr Tick had recently
insisted was played whenever he held assembly.
The general chatter in the hall died out.

'First of all,' he announced in his best
headmaster voice, 'I would like to thank Mrs
Tick for visiting the school and helping us all

by searching our hair for any sign of the head-lice infestation.'

He began to applaud, but neither the pupils nor staff shared his enthusiasm. They each remembered the pain they had felt at the hands of Granny Tick and grumbled unhappily.

Mrs Tick reached into the leather medical bag that sat at her feet and pulled out a metal nit comb that glinted in the light. Suddenly the applause grew in volume, punctuated only by the sound of Mr Downe screaming 'You'll never take me alive!' and crashing out through the rear doors.

'Is there anything you'd like to say?' Mr Tick asked his mother.

The large woman shook her head. 'You seem to have it covered, Dickie,' she said, at which the hall erupted in laughter.

The headmaster struggled to quieten the school down again. As the last few titters died away, he gestured to where Alexander was sitting with James and Lenny. 'I would also like to thank my son, Alexander, for leading the nits out of the school with his excellent, and previously unrecognised, musical abilities!'

Lenny pushed Alexander to his feet as the applause began.

'But it wasn't really me,' the headmaster's son whispered down to his friends as he stood and nervously took a bow.

'Accept the applause,' said James. 'It won't be long before you're annoying us all again with your jokes. Enjoy this brief moment of popularity!'

Alexander looked around the hall at all the pupils and staff who believed they had witnessed him leading the zombie nits away from the school. Slowly, a smile crept over his face and, before long, he was shaking hands with those around him.

'You know,' he said, as the clapping faded away, 'this reminds me of the man who took his dog to the vet . . .'

James and Lenny grabbed hold of Alexander's jumper and pulled him down. 'Don't push it!' warned James.

'Finally,' said Mr Tick, 'most of the credit for ridding the school of the head lice should really go to me!'

The pupils and staff exchanged glances and began to murmur angrily at the headmaster's words.

Mr Tick continued. 'It was me who invited Mrs Tick here to comb your heads for lice and, yes, it was me who ordered the special shampoo that was handed out to you all to help cleanse yourselves. Feel free to thank me!'

Mr Tick stretched out his hands to receive the gratitude of the school but all he felt was pain as a pencil was thrown from the back of the hall and pinged off his ear.

Clamping two fingers over his exposed nostrils, the headmaster stared down at the furious expressions of both the pupils and staff and thought fast.

'In order to celebrate the departure of the nits, morning lessons are cancelled and there will be a party held out on the sports field!' he announced.

A cheer went up around the hall as everyone leapt to their feet and rushed for the exits. Mr Tick sighed, pleased that he had averted yet another school disaster.

As the last few children left the hall, he sighed again. His nose and toe still ached from the battering they had taken the day before, and he hadn't managed to convince the stubborn Solitguy that they should replay the disputed solitaire match. Still, today looked as though it was going to be better.

Suddenly, an arm grabbed him from behind and a steel comb flashed into view. 'Stand perfectly still, Dickie!' hissed his mother's voice. 'Something just moved in your hair!'

Out on the sports field, Mr Drew hooked up a sound system and began to play music for the partying pupils.

'So, do you think the ghosts will try to attack the school again?' asked Lenny.

'Who knows?' replied James. 'Although I can't see them giving up that easily.'

'At least one of them is on our side, though,' added Alexander. 'That one with the flute. He led the zombie nits off down the stairs to the caretaker's room and, presumably, into the sewers.'

'Maybe there's hope for St Sebastian's yet,' mused James. 'And he did look a lot like you.'

Alexander shook his head. 'Couldn't see it myself,' he said. 'He was far too skinny for a start.'

'Too skinny!' exclaimed Lenny grabbing his friend by the elbow. 'Look at you! Your arms are like two bits of wet string with knots in the middle!'

'Well, some of us are designed for more academic pursuits,' snapped Alexander, pulling his arm away. 'Even if I couldn't come up with a solution to the nit problem.'

'Ah,' smiled James. 'But everyone in the school *thinks* you came up with the solution! It's almost the same thing.'

Alexander shrugged. 'I suppose so,' he said, as everyone around the friends began to pull off their hats and wigs and throw them in the air.

Within seconds, the sports field looked like the closing moments of some bizarre graduation ceremony.

'I wonder who he is,' said Alexander.

'Who?' asked James.

'The ghost,' replied Alexander. 'The one who looks like me.' He stared into space for a moment, thinking. 'I'd like to get to know a ghost,' he said. 'It would be great to have him for a friend.'

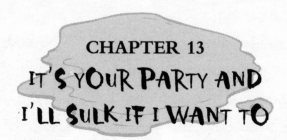

CHAPTER 13
IT'S YOUR PARTY AND
I'LL SULK IF I WANT TO

Edith Codd leant back against her upturned
barrel, ignored the party going on around her,
and sulked. She'd hardly spoken at all since she'd
been beaten back into the sewers the day before
by the tide of zombie nits and the music from
William's bone flute.

'She's got a face like the back end of a
donkey!' sang the children of the choir, as
Bertram Ruttle led a conga line of musicians
past Edith on their third lap of the amphitheatre.
All around, the plague-pit ghosts clapped along.

118

The music, however, was difficult to hear.
Since the zombie nits had arrived under the
school, chaos had reigned. After trying to bite
the ghosts for food and realising that not one
of them contained a single drop of blood, the

nits had turned their attentions to the sewer rats instead. And each time a rat was bitten, it let out a piercing squeak.

Before long, the sewer pipes were filled with an orchestra of angry rodents, each squeaking and squealing as it was bitten over and over again. Ambrose Harbottle was doing a roaring trade in leeches as the ghosts searched for something to jam into their ears to block out the noise.

The contented leech merchant sat back in his seat and watched as the Plague Pit Junior Ghost Band began another circle of the amphitheatre, a tide of rats and nits trailing after the musicians.

'This is my favourite bit!' he shouted to William over the noise of the rats. 'The line that goes "Her teeth look like she's dropped them down the loo"!'

Much to William's amazement, Ambrose jumped to his feet and began to dance to the music.

William stood and turned his bone flute over in his hands. For some reason, the zombie nits had

stopped following him once he'd reached the
sewers and splashed through a few puddles. Maybe
it hadn't been the music that had attracted them
after all. Still, whatever it was, he had saved the
school and, most importantly, his friends.

From the far side of the amphitheatre, Edith
watched the young ghost as he smiled at each
of the singing, skipping children.

'Come to me, William,' she whispered, trying
to look as unhappy as possible. 'I know you can't
bear to see anyone upset.'

By concentrating very hard, the old ghost
managed to squeeze out one ectoplasmic tear.
It glinted in the dim light, catching William's
eye. He hurried over as Edith struggled to hide
her grin; the plan was working.

'Are you OK?' William asked.

Edith shrugged, dramatically. 'All I wanted was
a bit of peace and quiet!' she moaned. '*Now* look
at the place.'

'They're just having fun,' said William. 'It's only a couple of days until the anniversary of the Great Fire of Grimesford. You could just say that the party started early this year.'

A wicked smile crept over Edith's face. 'I started that fire,' she admitted. 'The family in the room above mine wouldn't keep the noise down, so I pushed a burning rag under their door.'

'Was anyone hurt?' asked William, alarmed.

Edith shook her head. 'It holds the record for the largest fire without a single casualty,' she said. 'But the smell of burning food attracted rats from miles around, and they brought the plague to town.'

She gazed around the amphitheatre at the partying ghosts. 'It's my fault they all caught the Black Death,' she sighed, hoping that her unhappy mood would continue to fool William. 'My fault they're all buried here. I just want to make things more comfortable for them.' She sighed hard, keeping one eye on the young ghost.

'I'm sure they know that,' smiled William as the choir skipped past again, happily singing, 'She's as crazy as an old hag can become!'

'Oh, I wish those rats would be quiet!' groaned Edith, as the zombie nits attacked their rodent hosts again, and another series of high-pitched squeals echoed around the cavern.

'Here,' said William, 'this might help.'

Gripping the bone flute in his hands, he snapped the instrument in half and jammed each piece into one of Edith's ears.

'That's a bit better,' said the older ghost. William stood and made to leave.

'Where are you going?' asked Edith.

William shrugged. 'I thought I'd head up to the school and sit in on a few of the lessons,' he said. 'I don't understand what they're talking about most of the time, but I like being there with the pupils.'

Edith nodded and watched as the young ghost wandered away.

'William!' she called after him. The boy
stopped and turned. 'Thank you,' said Edith.

As William left the noise of the amphitheatre
behind and entered the sewer pipe that would
eventually lead him up to the boys' toilets, he
pulled a confused face. 'Could it really be that

Edith isn't that bad after all?' he asked himself.

Back in the amphitheatre, Edith waited until William had vanished from sight before pulling the pieces of bone flute from her ears and crushing them in her hands.

'That's it, young Scroggins,' she hissed. 'Start to feel sorry for me and eventually you'll begin to like me. Before long, you'll be my friend, and then I'll bring St Sebastian's School crashing down – with your unwitting help!'

'When she smiles she resembles a warthog, Licking poo from a thistle plant!' sang the choir as they passed the snarling old ghost again.

Angrily, Edith reached into the pile of bones at her side, plucked out a section of spine and threw it at the happy, dancing children.

A voice echoed out above the noise of the squeaking rats: 'Hey, that's mine!'

In his office, Mr Tick whistled happily as he stood in his private bathroom and thought back over the solitaire game he had just won against Solitguy. RedKing212 was back!

Flushing the toilet, he turned to wash his hands in the basin and glanced in the mirror at the deep, red scratches lining his scalp. He made a mental note to spend less on his Mother's Day present that year.

As he turned to leave the bathroom, a sound echoed up through the plughole. It sounded like a scream; an agonised scream of someone whose dreams had been shattered yet again.

Shivering, Mr Tick quickly pulled open the bathroom door and rushed over to his desk, where he stubbed his toe again.

His scream was even louder than Edith's.

SURNAME: Carver

FIRST NAME: Gordon
(nickname: 'The Gorilla')

AGE: 13

HEIGHT: 1.75 metres

EYES: Blue

HAIR: Brown and spiky

LIKES: The crunch of bones; the sound of younger children crying; seeing fear in smaller people's eyes

DISLIKES: Having to think too hard - or at all, in fact; doing his homework; other people, especially anybody related to the headmaster

SPECIAL SKILL: Can flip a year-seven student upside-down and hold his head down a toilet in under ten seconds flat

INTERESTING FACT: Gordon is the terror of year seven, but he himself lives in fear of the even scarier year eleven bullies; rumour has it they can flush your head down a toilet before you've even noticed they're in the room

For more facts on Gordon Carver,
go to **www.too-ghoul.com**

Alexander Tick's
Joke File
(page 3,989)

Q Why did the whale cross the road?

A To get to the other tide!

Q Why do birds fly south for the winter?

A Cos it's easier than walking!

Q What are prehistoric monsters called when they sleep?

A A dino-snores!

Q Why do idiots eat biscuits?

A Because they're crackers!

Q What kind of key opens a banana?

A A mon-key!

Nitty Nora's NIT TEST

Is your bonce covered in ZOMBIE NITS?

 1 How would you describe your haircut?

a. Short back and sides
b. Trendy and spiky
c. Seething with smelly bugs and goo

 2 What happens when you comb your hair?

a. It looks nice and neat
b. Some of your hair wax slops out
c. Your comb gets covered in bite marks

 3 How often do you wear a hat?

a. When it's really cold outside
b. When you're hair's too mucky to show other people
c. Every day – it stops the monsters biting

FOR MORE QUIZZES, VISIT **www.too-ghoul.com**

4. Does your scalp ever itch?

   a. Never – it's far too clean!

   b. Sometimes, when it's a bit sweaty

   c. Can't . . . answer . . . TOO . . . ITCHY . . . AAARGH!

5. Do grown-ups ever ruffle your hair?

   a. All the time – grown-ups love me

   b. Only when I score a good goal in football

   c. Never – an uncle tried it once, but he lost a finger

6. Do you have any pets?

   a. Yes, a hamster

   b. Yes, a smelly dog

   c. Are you joking? The animals on my head are quite enough!

How did you score?

Mostly As: Your clean hair could be in a shampoo advert.

Mostly Bs: You might have a few nits. But they aren't zombies.

Mostly Cs: You have zombie nits – SHAVE YOUR HEAD!

Nit-Charming Songs

Get a friend to play a medieval
bone flute while you sing these songs
and you'll soon be nit-free!

There was a young nit called Ritchie,
Who made heads exceedingly itchy.
He wanted to grow,
But his mother said 'no,
You're a nit - you'll always be titchy!'

A boy found some nits in his hair,
And it came as a bit of a scare!
He smothered them flat,
With a ridiculous hat,
But everyone knew they were there!

There once was a sporty young nit,
Who loved to keep himself fit.
He ran up and down hairs,
Cos there weren't any stairs,
On the head where he kept his sports kit.

A boy was slopping on lotion,
So his nits quickly sprang into motion.
But he had the last laugh,
He was sat in the bath,
Which to nits is as big as an ocean!

Can't wait for the next book in the series?
Here's a sneak preview of

FRENCH FRIGHTS

available now from all good bookshops,
or **www.too-ghoul.com**

CHAPTER 1
LOST IN TRANSLATION

James chewed on his pen, frowning.

'I can't do this!' he groaned. He threw the pen down on to the desk with a clatter.

Alexander looked up. He'd written three pages of a letter to his French pen pal already. Unlike James's scribbles, Alexander's page was neat and tidy, just like him.

'Here, James,' said Alexander, holding out a huge, leather-bound book, 'you can use my French dictionary. I got it for my birthday last year. I was really excited, because I'd always wanted . . .'

135

'Only you'd ask for a dictionary for your birthday!' James spluttered. 'Thanks, though. I'm having real trouble with this letter,' he sighed, grabbing the book from his friend and beginning to leaf through it.

It was Monday morning, and Madame Dupont – St Sebastian's French teacher – had instructed her year-sevens to fill their pen pals in on their latest news. She liked using the double lesson first thing on a Monday morning for this, as it meant she could ease her way in to the new week by drinking strong black coffee and reading her French newspaper in peace. She imagined she was sitting in a café in Paris rather than in her stuffy classroom at St Sebastian's.

Alexander signed his letter with a flourish and leant back in his chair, flexing his knuckles and stretching. James looked up.

'Well, that's this month's letter to Isabelle sorted out,' smiled Alexander. 'I can't *wait* to hear back from her. I've asked her lots of questions about the French government. She mentioned that her father works in an incredibly interesting department that organises payments for farmers –'

'Stick?' James interrupted.

'Yes, James?'

'Some of us haven't finished. And exciting as I am *sure* Isabelle's dad's job sounds – *not!* – I have to get this done before break time.' He scrubbed at his hair with frustration, leaving it sticking out like a punky hedgehog.

'Sorry, James! Here – let me help,' Alexander replied, leaning over to see what James had written. His brow furrowed. He scratched his head.

'It gives me the creeps when you scratch like that. Makes me think there are zombie nits on your bonce!' shuddered James.

'Have no fear, I'm a nit-free zone!' declared Alexander. He looked at James's letter and started to laugh.

'What's so funny?' James asked, frowning.

'Erm . . . did you mean to say "I like to ride my fish committee?"' Alexander spluttered.

Madame Dupont looked up from her newspaper. 'Alexandre? Is there a problem?'

'No, no – just helping the less fortunate!' Alexander giggled.

Madame Dupont smiled. 'Very well, Alexandre! Carry on!' She took a slurp of her coffee and went back to her newspaper.

James poked Alexander. 'What are you going on about? I was just telling Zac about my skateboard. I even used your stupid dictionary. I looked up "skate", then I looked up "board" and I put them together to make "skateboard". Simple. So I don't know why you're getting your knickers in a twist.'

'Well, you looked up "skate" and got the word for a type of flat fish, like a ray. Then you looked up "board" and you got the type of board that's a committee – like the board of school governors. Mind you, in a way, you're not far off the mark . . . when Dad talks to the governors I've seen them opening and closing their mouths like fish . . .'

'Oh, this is just stupid!' James snorted. 'I'll just draw a picture of me on my skateboard instead.'

'But Madame Dupont wants us to –' Alexander began. He was silenced by a glare from James. He swallowed hard and turned to Lenny, who was attaching some fluff to his letter with a piece of sticky tape.

'What's that?' Alexander asked.

'It was stuck in the zip of my pencil case. It's a clump of fur off our cat Cleo. She likes to sleep in my schoolbag, where it's dark and warm. Sometimes she leaves bits of herself behind . . .' He rummaged about in his bag and brought out a bent whisker. 'See!' He taped that to his letter too.

'OK . . . but why are you sticking it to your letter?' asked Alexander.

'Well, I was telling my pen pal, Manu, about the things my pets have been getting up to. I told him about the time my hamster escaped and hid in Mum's jewellery box. When she opened the lid, there was Leo wearing one of her bracelets like a necklace! I can't understand why she screamed. She scared the life out of him. And I also told him about the time Pooza the rabbit –'

'*Pooza?*' Alexander interrupted. 'What kind of name is that?!'

'Well, my mum said I should give my animals names that suit their personalities and habits,' Lenny smiled. 'And that rabbit poos – a *lot*. His cage is always full of piles of rabbit raisins. I have to clear him out twice a week – so that's how he earnt his name!'

'*Ewww* – too much information!' Alexander laughed, screwing up his nose.

'Anyway, I was just telling Manu about how Cleo likes to sleep in my schoolbag, when I suddenly had an idea. I wanted Manu to understand all about my pets, so that's why I stuck a bit of fluff on my letter.'

'Hey – it's a good job Pooza's not here. I don't think Manu would have liked rabbit raisins taped to his letter!'

The boys tried to stifle their laughter.

Madame Dupont looked up at that moment, but they were saved by the school bell. Everyone began to cram books into their schoolbags.

Madame Dupont clapped her hands to get attention. 'Wait a minute, please, everyone! I have an exciting announcement to make!'

'Free *pain au chocolat* for everyone?' wondered Alexander, hopefully.

'Don't be daft, Stick! What use would a chocolate pan be? It'd be as useless as a chocolate teapot. No good for cooking . . .' Lenny frowned.

'No, not a chocolate pan – *pain au chocolat*!

We had them on holiday last year. They're flaky pastry with chocolate chips – yum!' Alexander smiled, wistfully. His tummy rumbled.

'I have arranged a pupil exchange with L'Ecole de St Martin, your pen pals' school in Poubelle! You will all finally get to meet your French friends – next week!' trilled Madame Dupont, beaming at her pupils with excitement.

The boys looked at each other in silence. Then they grinned.

'Wow! A school trip to France!' cried James. 'Brilliant! I've always fancied . . .'

'Sorry, James. We are going nowhere. The students from L'Ecole de St Martin are to come here,' Madame Dupont smiled.

James deflated like a burst balloon.

'Aww, Madame Dupont . . .!' he moaned.

'I shall give you all more details very soon! Now I must go to make arrangements . . .' And with a waft of her chiffon scarf – leaving a trail of expensive perfume in her wake – the French mistress swept out of the classroom.

James turned to Lenny and Alexander. 'You can always trust a teacher to suck the fun out of things!' he grumbled.

'Cheer up, James! It'll be great. We'll be able to show them around Grimesford . . .' said Alexander.

'And Manu will be able to meet my pets!' Lenny grinned.

'Hmm, well, I suppose I'll be able to show Zac my skateboard. He could even come to the skatepark,' said James, perking up a bit.

'You know, I've got a theory why teachers suck all the fun out of things,' said Alexander. 'Do you want to hear it?'

James sighed and crossed his arms. 'No, I don't – but I've got a horrible feeling I'm going to anyway.'

'Because somewhere along the line they've been crossed with vampires.'

'Eh?' James grunted. 'I'm not sure I get where this is going . . .'

'And do you know what you get if you cross a teacher with a vampire?'

James and Lenny silently exchanged puzzled glances.

'Someone who likes to do a lot of blood tests!' Alexander laughed.

His friends rolled their eyes and groaned, and the boys pushed and jostled with each other as they headed out of the classroom to the playground.